The Underpants

The Underpants

A Play by Carl Sternheim

ADAPTATION BY STEVE MARTIN

AN IMPRINT OF HYPERION

NEW YORK

"The Underpants" was originally produced at Classic Stage Company, New York, Barry Edelstein, Artistic Director, on March 21, 2002.

Book design by Lisa Stokes

ISBN: 0-7868-8824-5

Hyperion books are available for special promotions and premiums. For details contact Hyperion Special Markets, 77 West 66th Street, 11th floor, New York, New York 10023, or call 212-456-0100.

FIRST EDITION

10 9 8 7 6 5 4 3 2 1

In other adaptations I have done—*Cyrano de Bergerac* became the film *Roxanne,* and *Silas Marner* became the film *A Simple Twist of Fate*—I have come to understand that however true I intend to remain to the original text, the adaptation is continuously influenced, altered, and redefined by modern times. Each time, the process has taken me through the stages of a failing marriage: fidelity, transgression, and finally separation.

The job seems easy at first. It feels as though all one has to do is update a few sentences, modernize a few references, and one is finished. But a nasty thing happens. One's own inherent presence in the current age intrudes. In a sociopolitical play like Sternheim's *The Underpants*, meanings change through time. What was relevant then is historical now. And what was tangential then can become central. I chose not to present the play as historical artifact. I decided to uncork the genie that Sternheim had placed in the bottle—the genie that makes the play relevant to our age. In doing so, I have had to subordinate some themes in the original, and emphasize others that, like Sternheim's sea serpent, lurked under the surface. Sternheim's play is ribald, satirical, self-referential, and quirky. I hope I have retained those elements and assured my place in heaven—I mean, served the playwright's intentions.

I would like to thank the Classic Stage Company, whose productions I have long admired, and specifically Barry Edelstein, who first brought the play to my attention.

STEVE MARTIN

The Underpants

Theo Maske: A burly, muscular fireplug with a buzz cut.

Louise Maske: Very pretty, mid-twenties, Theo's wife.

Gertrude Deuter: Forty-two, and a busybody.

Frank Versati: An elegant gentleman.

Benjamin Cohen: Sickly, thin, asthmatic.

Klinglehoff: An elderly man.

Dialogue in brackets indicates alternate lines for actors of different body types.

DUSSELDORF, *March 1910, Theo and Louise's flat. We see the combined living room/kitchen of an apartment. Two upstage doors allow us to see into two small bedrooms, one elevated several feet above the other on a landing. There is a bird in a cage. There is a sign placed in a high window: ROOM FOR RENT.*

THEO

This did not happen. It could not happen, yet it did!

LOUISE

No one even noticed.

THEO

In front of the neighbors, in front of strangers, and at the King's parade, for god's sake? The King himself could have seen you.

LOUISE

No one saw me.

THEO

So the story just spread itself.

LOUISE

It was nothing.

THEO

It was nothing? It was nothing? Tell me if this is nothing. In broad daylight, on a city street, you are standing out in public and your underpants fall down. I can't believe this happened to me!

LOUISE

It didn't happen to you.

THEO

But they will blame me. They will blame me for having a wife who is so distracted by staring out the window, who is so hypnotized by a canary in a cage, that she can't even tie a tiny knot in two slender cords. I'm sorry, but I am a responsible wage earner. *I* cannot have my underpants go flopping down because *I* must bring home six hundred taler a year plus bear the responsibility of renting out a room . . .

(He indicates a second bedroom.)

so we can put dinner on the table, clothe ourselves and keep the place heated.

LOUISE

The whole event lasted two seconds!

THEO

Haven't you heard? Time is relative.

(He references the newspaper.)

LOUISE

I pulled them up.

THEO

Please. Don't be graphic.

LOUISE

They were on tight. They fell.

THEO

Oh my god, what's going to happen to me? I'll be fired!
What about my income!

LOUISE

Oh, Theo.

THEO

Louise, everything in *my* world is running perfectly. But here
at home, how can the floor be so dirty, how can the clock not
be wound . . .

(*He indicates a clock on the mantel.*)

how can the dishes be so piled up, and how, I ask you how,
can your panties, in broad daylight, just fall down?

(*There are very few dishes in the sink,
and the apartment is quite clean.*)

LOUISE

You know me. You've known me since I was a little girl.

THEO

And?

LOUISE

You know that I like to dream.

THEO

Dream the dishes done.

LOUISE

You used to like my reveries.

THEO

In a girl, yes. There's nothing lovelier. There was nothing
better to do with all that free time but to lie around as pretty
as an orchid. But now you're a woman. Reality is here. It is
in this room, in the dust on the floor, in that dirty sink.

LOUISE

Oh, phooey. I keep the place nice.

THEO

(Calmer.)

Look how deeply affected I am.

LOUISE

Yes, you're very sensitive.

THEO

You know how I hate attention. A little attention and the
next thing you know I am out of a job. I am a government
clerk. *I* blend in. You know why I never buy you a pretty
dress, or hat or new coat?

LOUISE

Remind me.

                              THEO

Because you are much too attractive for a man in my posi-
tion. Your breasts, your legs, they draw the eyes. My job and
your appearance do not go together. Everyone notices you.
And it's your fault.

                              LOUISE

My fault?

                              THEO

The woman's fault, always.

                              LOUISE

Here we go again.

                              THEO

What are breasts? Harmless, utilitarian, lumps of flesh. But
you squeeze them into a sweater and mountains move.

                              LOUISE

I don't promote myself.

                              THEO

You don't have to. Flesh speaks to men from under coats,
under caftans, under furs, from igloos. There's always a small
voice calling: I am here.

                              LOUISE

Men can't be like that.

THEO

What if I lose my job . . .

LOUISE

Why would you lose your job?

THEO

I was told that his Royal Highness was in the parade.

LOUISE

He was passing at the very moment.

THEO

Oh!

LOUISE

But that's good. Everyone was looking at him, not me.

THEO

And suppose he hears about this fiasco? Suppose he hears I am one of his clerks? He discovers my section, my bureau, my name. The King cannot abide scandal. He will have to fire me. The next thing you know, we're out on the street! Poverty, shame, hunger.

LOUISE

All from a pair of underpants.

THEO

Don't underestimate the power of a glimpse of lingerie.

(After a pause . . .)

I'm exhausted.

LOUISE
How would like your wiener grilled?

THEO
Take the knife and slice it from tip to end. Not crossways like you usually do.

LOUISE

(With acrimony.)

One wiener, sliced from tip to end. My pleasure. And for dessert?

THEO
Peaches and whipped cream. Do we have some?

LOUISE
I could get some. From Gertrude.

THEO
Gertrude Deuter. The mouth who lives upstairs.

(He stands up and shakes his fist at the apartment above, where Gertrude lives.)

Nosy! Oh well.

(He glances at the newspaper on the kitchen table. Louise busies herself about the kitchen.)

Hmm. Reports of a monster in the Loch Ness. It baffles the scientists, and it bothers me. I do not need these little mysteries. The unexplainable makes me nervous. I have my home, and everything that comes in the door I understand. I don't have to worry that the faucet will spit fire. I do not have to worry that the bird will attack the dog. The clock will strike six when it is six and not seven. It is like me; it is my kind of clock.

(He picks up the paper again.)

Monsters in a lake. All is calm on the surface, but watch out for what's underneath. That's where the danger lies. Under. Under. Underpants!

(He throws down his paper, gets up.)

I'm going to go out and circulate around the town and catch wind of what people are saying. See if I still have an income. Please have dinner ready when I get back.

LOUISE

Do you feel better now?

THEO

Only when I think how good life has been up until today.

(He leaves. Louise follows him onto the stairway landing, until he is gone. Then she calls from the window.)

Gertrude!

GERTRUDE

(From above.)

I've been listening, Louise.

LOUISE

Then you know about my little accident?

GERTRUDE

(Coming down the stairs.)

I heard some gossip on the street.

LOUISE

How much did you hear?

GERTRUDE

Should I come down?

LOUISE

Please.

(Gertrude enters immediately. She's been listening at the door.)

What did you hear?

GERTRUDE

I heard it wasn't so bad . . . They were clean cotton, neat and perfectly ironed.

LOUISE

Well, of course.

GERTRUDE

And very few people know the story.

LOUISE

Where did you hear it?

GERTRUDE

It was announced at the train station. How did it happen?

LOUISE

I was trying to see the King. I was on a bench, up on tiptoes.

(Louise illustrates.)

GERTRUDE

It slims the waist.

(They begin to giggle. Gertrude joins in, running her hands along her own waist.)

LOUISE

Suddenly I felt my underpants around my ankles.

GERTRUDE

A welcome breeze in the netherworld.

LOUISE

Gertrude!

GERTRUDE

They say you looked lovely. I heard a couple of men turned their heads quite a lot.

LOUISE

I kept my dignity. I stepped out of them, bent down and swooped them under my shawl. Like lightning.

GERTRUDE

Tomorrow, everyone will say the whole thing was a perfectly planned piece of coquetry.

LOUISE

Oh God. My husband can't stand it when people talk.

GERTRUDE

Well, he'll just have to get used to a lot of things. Like where the sun shines is where people want to walk.

LOUISE

What do you mean?

GERTRUDE

Like a pretty girl turns heads and there's nothing he can do about it.

LOUISE

He's just being a man.

GERTRUDE

He's not all men. There are better ones.

LOUISE

(Sternly changing the subject.)

Please, Gertrude. Do you have any whipped cream?

GERTRUDE

I do. I'll get it. I heard him.

(Cautious.)

Louise, haven't you been married about a year?

LOUISE

A year this Sunday.

GERTRUDE

And?

LOUISE

And?

GERTRUDE

The patter of little feet?

LOUISE

Oh.

GERTRUDE

Can that be just chance? Or is it your husband is not doing his job?

LOUISE

He works hard.

GERTRUDE

I mean his job between the sheets.

LOUISE

Gertrude!

GERTRUDE

I'll get your whipped cream.

(Gertrude exits. Noise from offstage, then a man gently knocks on the door. He is Frank Versati, an elegant gentleman. He enters through the open door.)

VERSATI

Excuse me?

LOUISE

Yes?

VERSATI

I saw you have a room for rent.

LOUISE

Yes, we do.

VERSATI

We?

LOUISE

Yes, my husband and I.

VERSATI

Of course. But the room is still for rent?

LOUISE

Yes. But my husband is out.

GERTRUDE

(From offstage.)

Louise!

VERSATI

I'll have a look around the property and come back.

LOUISE

Your name?

*(He vanishes up the stairwell. Gertrude appears, with a bowl of
whipped cream.)*

GERTRUDE

Whipped cream. And more. I've been thinking. Your husband is shirking his duty. You deserve something in you at
night besides sauerkraut. I'll show you a few tricks, and give
you hints for looking good. I'm going to help you turn him
into a ravenous beast. Take this . . .

(She hands Louise the whipped cream.)

I can't wait to work on you.

(She exits. Versati reappears.)

LOUISE

My husband is not back yet.

VERSATI

You must have some authority.

LOUISE

Would you like to know the rate?

VERSATI

No.

LOUISE

Oh. Would you like to see the room?

VERSATI

That's not necessary.

LOUISE

You would rent a room without seeing it?

VERSATI

Yes.

LOUISE

Why?

VERSATI

Because . . . because . . .

(Blurts it out.)

Your underpants! This morning, on the Grand Boulevard.

LOUISE

(Shocked.)

Oh my god! Who are you?

VERSATI

I am a poet. Unpublished—I am proud to say—but one who has now found his muse.

LOUISE

Please!

VERSATI

I will explain. By metaphor. No, by simile. No, I will not beat around the bush. Oh my god, what an inappropriate allusion. I am not the master of my soul. Though a few hours ago I was. It seems I am engulfed by the rising tide of my own humors . . .

(He is pleased by his metaphor.)

What a beautiful line . . . where is my pen!

(He can't find it.)

Damn. Society's loss.

(Back to her.)

You see I believe in miracles, and I finally had one appear to me under a linden tree. There you were, bathed in sunlight, with panicked eyes and a quivering body and there I was, shaken by life. A momentous crossroads. In those few seconds, when you bent down and collected your underpants, you tore my heart from the things that I thought I loved, and fixed it only on you.

(Louise is breathless.)

Ah, silence. Good. For silence is devotion.

(He moves toward her.)

LOUISE
I . . . I . . . don't know what to say.

VERSATI

(He kneels on his upstage knee, downstage knee hiding his groin.)

Then let me speak: From this day on, I will desire you with all the strength of my soul. Unwavering, disavowing all others.

LOUISE
Please, stand up.

VERSATI
I cannot stand, for my veins are stiff with certainty.

LOUISE

(She looks between his legs, steps back, shocked.)

For god's sake, if my husband comes!

VERSATI

The room you have for rent. How much is it?

LOUISE

Fifteen taler.

VERSATI

I'll take it. The discussion is over.

LOUISE

Who would believe an elegant gentleman living in this neighborhood?

VERSATI

I'll dress as a laborer. A wealthy, gentleman hod carrier.

LOUISE

And you would live here?

VERSATI

In the extra room.

LOUISE

What about my husband?

VERSATI

If he comes, just introduce us. I'm renting the room.

LOUISE

And you are . . . ?

VERSATI

Versati. Franklin, Angelo, "The Cat," Luigi, Versati the second. Sorry, the third.

LOUISE

You should get up. He'll be coming back soon.

VERSATI

Between the sound of his key in the lock and the opening of the door I will be fleet like Jupiter. Wait, Jupiter is not fleet. Make that Mercury.

LOUISE

Get up!

VERSATI

You'll agree, then?

LOUISE

I . . .

(They play the pause.)

VERSATI

In the ellipsis sounds a yes!

LOUISE

But my husband!

VERSATI

Think of him as a necessary part of the triangle. You are the flint, I am the fire, and he is the wet piece of wood. I'll be back.

(He exits, leaving the door ajar. Louise goes into the guest room. The stage is bare. We hear a knock, and the door swings open from the force. Enter Klinglehoff. He looks around, surveying the place.)

KLINGLEHOFF

Hello?

(After a moment, he exits. Louise reappears with a ladder. She climbs a ladder halfway to a high window. Gertrude enters. She looks around.)

GERTRUDE

Louise?

LOUISE

Up here.

GERTRUDE

In the clouds. As usual.

LOUISE

What do you mean?

GERTRUDE

Who was he?

LOUISE

Who was who?

GERTRUDE

Who was that gentleman?

LOUISE

How do you know there was a gentleman here?

GERTRUDE

I'm not deaf.

LOUISE

And obviously not nosy.

GERTRUDE

I was cleaning my floor, and you know how when you're scrubbing you put your ear on the floor for leverage? . . . Oh look, he was practically orating. What did he want?

LOUISE

What do you think?

GERTRUDE

(Dreamy.)

Ah. Wanted by a gentleman. I'd give ten years of my life. Where did he meet you?

                    LOUISE

He saw me this morning.

                    GERTRUDE

In all your glory.

                    LOUISE

Bending over to retrieve them.

                    GERTRUDE

And he sprang like a tiger.

                    LOUISE

He was out of control.

                    GERTRUDE

Shook to his roots. And you responded.

                    LOUISE

Of course not. But he's renting the room from us.

                    GERTRUDE

So your ascent to the heights makes sense.

(Louise plucks the "For Rent" sign out of the window. Gertrude looks up her dress.)

Ah. I see what all the fuss was about.

LOUISE

Gertrude, you're naughty.

(She comes down the ladder.)

GERTRUDE

Oh my god. I'm going to have an affair.

LOUISE

What do you mean?

GERTRUDE

Because I live through you, and you are going to have a lover.

LOUISE

No!

GERTRUDE

I'll see to it. I'm going to be your fairy godmother. Here's what we're going to do: You should dress so your husband only sees his old Cinderella. But underneath . . . I'll make you a pair of panties that will raise his flag higher and higher . . .

LOUISE

How can you say that? I'm married.

GERTRUDE

So was Catherine the Great and she slept with a horse.

LOUISE

I can't!

GERTRUDE

But a god is here to claim you. You can't say no!

LOUISE

My husband would kill me if he found out.

GERTRUDE

I'll see that he never does. A little smoke can blind a thousand eyes.

LOUISE

I refuse.

GERTRUDE

It's too late. You're already thinking about it. Whenever you sat in front of that window, looking out, dreaming, you were thinking of it. When you stare at the bird in that cage, you're seeing yourself. Why hasn't your husband used the year he's had with you to make your blood flow faster? Why aren't you pregnant?

LOUISE

He says we can't afford a child. We have to save up.

GERTRUDE

While he saves up, you look out the window for a real lover.

LOUISE

(Confessing.)

Except for our wedding night, I'd still be a virgin. He keeps saying, six hundred taler a year.

GERTRUDE

I want that gentleman to be your lover.

LOUISE

Oh my god, the wieners!

GERTRUDE

Yes, every last one of them!

LOUISE

(She opens the stove.)

Our dinner! It's burned!

GERTRUDE

Oh. I have some sausages cooking upstairs. I'll give them to you.

LOUISE

You'll save me.

GERTRUDE

I'll be right back.

(She runs up the stairs. Louise is alone. She goes to the window, looks out. She opens it, and takes a long deep breath in front of it. She then stands center stage and deliberately rises on her tiptoes. Nothing happens. She rises again, trying to see if her underpants will fall down. They don't.)

LOUISE

(To herself.)

How did they fall?

(She tries again.)

Unrepeatable. It must have been the Lord who did it.

(Gertrude appears with a pan full of sausage.)

GERTRUDE

Here. It's almost ready, just put it in the stove and heat it up.

LOUISE

How can I thank you?

GERTRUDE

By listening. I've wanted to tell you this for a long time. Your husband is a loud, clanking machine. Get in his way and he'll run you over. But like all hot-air machines, you can hear him coming. So I'll be your lookout.

LOUISE

(Considering.)

You make it seem so easy.

GERTRUDE

Aren't you tired of him wagging his finger at you?

LOUISE

Oh, the thought of having a lover. Someone who wants me. Someone who swims in my flesh and drowns in my breasts. Someone to whom I am ... aromatic.

(Then ...)

Will you help me?

GERTRUDE

Only if you follow my advice. When your husband's home, you're the dutiful wife. But between the hours of nine and three, when your husband is at work, you know what's going to be happening to you? Ah ...

LOUISE

Go get the fabric!

GERTRUDE

Your husband's only getting what he deserves.

LOUISE

Gertrude, one thing. Don't judge me.

GERTRUDE

How can I judge? My heart races along with yours.

LOUISE

I'm blushing.

GERTRUDE

Like being a girl again.

LOUISE

How do I know he'll want me?

GERTRUDE

Just wait till you make your entrance in the panties I make for you.

LOUISE

You've opened a dam inside me!

(They giggle vociferously and celebrate, hugging each other.)

GERTRUDE

Oh, and one other thing . . .

(She produces a vial of fluid.)

For safety.

LOUISE

What is it?

GERTRUDE

It's a sleeping mixture from the chemist. For your husband. In case you want to make a night visit.

LOUISE

Does it work?

GERTRUDE

Remember that weekend when I was gone? This is where
I was.

(She holds up the vial.)

One teaspoon and he's a hibernating bear.

(She takes the vial and puts it in a cabinet. There are loud footsteps
coming from outside.)

Shh. Your husband's coming.

LOUISE

How can you tell?

GERTRUDE

It's either him or a Clydesdale. You see what a good sentry
I am?

LOUISE

Here quick, set out the forks.

(She stops to dream.)

I remember seeing a painting of a woman on a sofa swathed
in a veil. A man stands over her, parting her legs with his
foot . . .

GERTRUDE

He's coming!

LOUISE

I imagine myself as that woman, giving up everything to him. He lies between my legs . . .

GERTRUDE

Stop!

LOUISE

He is above me . . . he looks into my eyes and says . . .

(*The door opens. Theo walks in.*)

THEO

Is the sausage in the oven?

GERTRUDE

Oh my god.

LOUISE

It's almost ready.

(*Gertrude hurries out. She bumps into Benjamin Cohen, 35, thin, asthmatic. He is with Theo.*)

THEO

What did you do with the "For Rent" sign?

LOUISE

Good news, the room is rented.

COHEN

The room's rented?! Oy.

THEO

What?

COHEN

Aye. I said aye, yi yi, the room's rented.

THEO

(To Cohen.)

Don't worry. I gave you my word.

COHEN

Yes, you did.

THEO

(To Louise.)

How much?

LOUISE

Fifteen taler.

THEO

Including?

LOUISE

Not including.

THEO

(To Cohen.)

How about fifteen taler, without.

COHEN

Without what?

THEO

Without coffee. The way she makes it, it's not something you want, believe me.

(To Louise.)

I wish you had spoken to me first. Now look at the mess. I only left the house in the first place because of you, and see what happens, trouble.

(To Cohen.)

Look, I don't want to be greedy. "Who" is just as important to me as "How much." What do you do, Herr . . . ?

COHEN

Cohen.

THEO

Cohen?

                    COHEN

Cohen.

                    THEO

Jewish?

                    COHEN

No.

                    THEO

Look into the light.

    (Theo grabs him by the face and turns him into the light.)

                    COHEN

That's Cohen with a *K*.

                    THEO

You understand I really don't mind.

                    COHEN

Yes, I can tell.

                    THEO

Well then . . .

            (Shakes Cohen's hand.)

So. You were going to pay twelve taler for the room.

                    COHEN

With coffee.

THEO

And now, there's someone who can take the room for fifteen.
Put yourself in my shoes.

COHEN

I hope that arithmetic won't compromise your promise to me.

THEO

Of course not. How could I be a welsher? This country produced Schiller, it produced Luther, and it produced me.

COHEN

And Wagner!

THEO

And me!

COHEN

And Wagner!

THEO

And me! You're a good German. The deal is done!

(They shake hands.)

Stay and have a bite with us.

LOUISE

But . . .

COHEN

I would love to.

LOUISE

But we have another renter.

THEO

I have a plan. But first, tell us about yourself, Cohen with a *K*.

COHEN

My parents died young. Thus, I work with my hands.

THEO

Nothing wrong in that.

COHEN

I've been three years in the same job. I'm a barber.

THEO

I respect the workingman.

COHEN

At night, every penny I can spare is for Wagner. I've seen *Lohengrin* three times.

THEO

Good man.

COHEN

One is transported.

THEO

Do you exercise?

COHEN

Not a lick. My health is poor.

(He coughs, slaps his chest.)

THEO

What's wrong with your health?

COHEN

Well, there's no specific diagnosis. My mother was delicate and she never ate well. My father drank more than he should.

THEO

Feel my thigh.

(He gets up, flexes his thigh. Cohen feels it, tentatively.)

COHEN

Massive.

THEO

Feel these.

(He flexes his biceps.)

COHEN

Enormous.

THEO

I could lift you in the air a hundred times. You stay with us, we'll feed you, give you some weight.
[If the actor's heavy, tone.]

LOUISE

Shouldn't we think about it?

THEO

Give him a cigar to celebrate.

LOUISE

We're out. You were going to get some.

THEO

That's right, this morning. Your scandal made me forget. Meanwhile, I have a solution to this whole mess. You see, we could, if it were for a long lease, put up a wooden screen and create two rooms out of one.

LOUISE

I don't know if he'd do that.

COHEN

(To Theo.)

You've given me your word.

THEO

My god, you will have your room, Herr Cohen. I'll get some cigars for the closing of the deal. Wait here.

(He exits. There is a moment's silence.)

COHEN

Well.

LOUISE

This location must be convenient. Do you work at the barbershop across the street?

COHEN

I work on Linden Street.

LOUISE

Linden Street? That's a half-hour walk.

COHEN

Yes, I know.

LOUISE

That's a hike every morning.

COHEN

It is a bit far.

LOUISE

This is a less expensive neighborhood.

COHEN

Not really.

LOUISE

Are you all right? You seem nervous.

COHEN

Nervous? Hahahahaha. I am a bit.

LOUISE

But why would you be nervous?

COHEN

Well. Interesting.

LOUISE

Is it?

COHEN

It's just that...

LOUISE

Yes...

COHEN

It's just that...

LOUISE

What?

COHEN

Underpants.

LOUISE

Pardon me?

COHEN

Today, this morning, when your underpants fell down. I couldn't believe what I was seeing. So naughty! I got so excited . . .

(Theo enters. Cohen instantly changes tone.)

And how often is the chimney swept?

THEO

Cigars to close the deal.

COHEN

I don't smoke.

THEO

No wonder you're so puny [unhealthy]. Cigars strengthen the body.

(He stands him up.)

See my rib cage? Room in there for everything. Air, perfume from the ladies, smoke.

(Instructs.)

Deep breath . . . arms out. Bend backwards.

(Cohen does. There's a knock at the door.)

Hold that pose. I'll get the door.

(Cohen holds the pose. Theo leaves to answer the door.)

LOUISE

(Quickly, to Cohen.)

How dare you come here!

COHEN

I had to.

LOUISE

Go away.

COHEN

I won't!

(Versati enters with Theo.)

THEO

(To Cohen, who still holds the pose.)

And relax.

VERSATI

...But I presented my application to your wife.

THEO

Yes, my wife told me that you were interested in the room. However, in the meantime, without knowing of your offer, I received an application from Herr Cohen, with a *K,* who comes from a good German family, and I rented it out.

VERSATI

But your wife accepted. It's a deal.

LOUISE

Herr Cohen was just saying that he wants to leave . . .

COHEN

I most certainly did not.

THEO

So what I was thinking was that we would divide the room. It's almost two rooms already. I'll close it off with furniture and a divider, and you could take your pick. Come on, I'll show you the space.

(Versati and Theo exit.)

LOUISE

I will tell my husband.

COHEN

I can't stop you. But if you do, I will tell him the real reason why that gentleman is renting a room in this house.

LOUISE

You know him?

COHEN

I do know him.

                    LOUISE
How well?

                    COHEN
Extremely well.

                    LOUISE
He's a friend?

                    COHEN
No.

                    LOUISE
A relative?

                    COHEN
No.

                    LOUISE
Then . . . ?

                    COHEN
I have colored his hair twice.

                    LOUISE
Really?

                    COHEN
He won't remember me, but I know all about him. I saw
him this morning, when your panties fell down. I was lying
on the ground only two steps away . . .

LOUISE

Two steps away, lying on the ground! That's disgusting.

COHEN

To me, it was paradise. If I saw what I think I saw . . . oh
please, let it be what I think I saw.

LOUISE

Herr Cohen!

COHEN

And just now, when I saw the look on Versati's face. I knew
that we wanted the same thing.

(Theo and Versati reenter.)

THEO

Herr Versati agrees. He'll pay fifteen taler, and not only that,
he only intends to use it for certain hours of the day.

VERSATI

(To Theo.)

I'll slip in and out without you knowing it.

THEO

And my wife, sir, has able hands and is willing to please a
person of your standing.

VERSATI

If you insist.

THEO

Louise, every morning, you will make his bed.

LOUISE

Yes, dear.

THEO

Well. Two new boarders. What could be more perfect?

(He goes to a drawer.)

Here are your keys. The facilities are upstairs. No flushing
after midnight, it arouses the cats. Oh, and as I am in the
civil service, I am obliged to ask you both if you are planning
to work against the government or undertake anything sub-
versive?

VERSATI

I am what you see.

COHEN

How could I be otherwise.

THEO

It makes me proud to know that there are still such honor-
able men in Germany.

COHEN

Then we start tonight.

VERSATI

Tonight!

THEO

(To Versati.)

And the contract will last a year.

VERSATI

Done.

(To Louise.)

Dear lady.

COHEN

(Leaving.)

Shalo ... lo ... lo ... lo ... la, la.

(Versati and Cohen exit.)

THEO

Well. Two paying boarders. We, my dear, are better off than we were this morning. Thank god your sluttishness has had no consequences.

LOUISE

I don't like the barber. He says he's sick. He'll bring his diseases into the house.

THEO

He's not sick. He's sickly. There's a difference.

LOUISE

But why have him in your home?

THEO

Twelve taler a month! Think of it, Louise.

(He starts to leave.)

Oh, and didn't you just laugh when the other one turned to you and said, "Dear lady"? To my little Louise who lost her panties?

(He begins to laugh; Louise is worried about Cohen.)

I mean didn't you just laugh? "Dear lady"? Ha ha ha ha.

LOUISE

(Aside.)

Oh Gertrude, what am I to do?

(Blackout.)

THE NEXT MORNING. *Lights up. Theo and Cohen enter from the bedroom.*

THEO

Well, Cohen, one night sleeping near the window and you've got a robust glow. I knew it would be good for you. Versati wanted to sleep next to the furnace, but it dries out the nasal passages.

COHEN

What do you know about this Versati?

THEO

The gentleman, as far as I can tell, is pursuing a personal affair.

COHEN

Ah, an affair.

THEO

No, a *personal* affair. Please use your words correctly. There's a big difference.

COHEN

You're very precise.

THEO

Of course. Not to be precise is to take the long way 'round. From nine in the morning to three in the afternoon I have official papers in front of me. How could I not be precise?

COHEN

I am the opposite. I have to keep my customers entertained. I have to keep blathering. Sense, nonsense, puns and anecdotes.

THEO

That's the difference between you and me. I am a realist. I face things as they are. You even lie to yourself about your own health. What time do you have to be at work?

                    COHEN
Not until ten.

                    THEO
Then go walking in the morning. Get some exercise.

                    COHEN
I'll get winded.

                    THEO
Only at first. Plus, you need to find out what's wrong with
you.

                    COHEN
Why?

                    THEO
So you know where you stand.

                    COHEN
If I found out what was wrong with me, I'd just get sicker
worrying about it. So of what use is the truth?

                    THEO
Good god, man, what good are lies?

                    COHEN
Everything around us is lies.

THEO

Are you crazy? Everything around us is lies? Your statement
is the only lie in this household.

COHEN

Nonsense. They are everywhere.

THEO

Where are there lies in this household? With Herr Versati?

COHEN

No doubt.

THEO

With my wife?

COHEN

Perhaps.

THEO

And you?

COHEN

Could be.

THEO

So you are not really a barber. You're a disguised baron, my
wife's lover, who has wormed his way in here.

COHEN

I beg your pardon!

THEO

A fellow of unimaginable strength, of glowing health, like a titan standing astride the river of masculinity.

(Louise enters from the bedroom.)

Louise, you can leave your bourgeois life behind you. Cohen here is a baron, your lover, and everything around us is a lie. Herr Cohen, you are a jester. You're going to make things very entertaining around here. I'm going out for some air. It builds the corpuscles. Come with me, Cohen, it'll do you good.

COHEN

I think I need to rest.

THEO

Like a titan astride the river of masculinity.

(He exits. Cohen's indignity fades.)

COHEN

He makes it so easy.

LOUISE

Makes what easy?

COHEN

It's amazing how trusting he is.

LOUISE

Until today, he had no reason not to be.

COHEN

His eyes will be opened one day.

LOUISE

By men he took into his house.

COHEN

With excuses that a kid could see through ... slip in and out ... a personal affair ... And you can't wait to sleep with Versati.

LOUISE

If you insult me I'll call back my husband.

COHEN

Call him. He's still on the stairs. And I'll tell him everything.

LOUISE

Why don't you leave?

COHEN

Do you think I can watch silently while another man conquers you? I can't allow it. When I saw you in the park, I wanted you like nothing else in my life. And when I found Versati here, overflowing with lust for you, my jealousy pulled me taut like a crossbow, and I knew I had to stop him. If I can't have you, neither will he.

LOUISE

When is it you have to go to work?

COHEN

You underestimate me, Frau Maske. You won't sleep with him.

LOUISE

You are a child.

COHEN

(Softening.)

It wasn't my fault what I saw. I'm being pulled along by it. You see, Frau Maske, I have been a solitary person, shunned almost all my life. But when I saw you in the park, I had a new companion: my desire. And suddenly I wasn't so alone.

LOUISE

I think I understand.

COHEN

I promise you, I will never transgress any boundary you set for me. And if you ever need protection from that brute, I would, to my last breath, stand by you.

LOUISE

(Slyly.)

Maybe, in time, we could become friends.

COHEN

And Herr Versati?

LOUISE

Oh please, he's a fop. I don't have any interest in him.

COHEN

I don't have much experience with women, so I don't know
if you're fooling me.

LOUISE

He might want me. But you're forgetting my part in the
matter. You think I can't see through this Don Juan? To
him, I'd just be an easy conquest. Do you think I'd give up
all this for a meaningless fling?

COHEN

But the way he looked at you, I thought you were . . .

LOUISE

He looked at me without permission.

COHEN

I will never look without permission. I will be undemanding,
and the smallest thing, a breath, will make me happy.

LOUISE

Maybe you and I will have a future.

COHEN

You're not fooling me?

LOUISE

Herr Cohen, I need you to go out and get some coffee.
Would you mind?

COHEN

Of course not.

LOUISE

You're such a gentleman.

(She kisses him on the cheek, then gets his scarf.)

You're not dressed for the weather. Here, it's threatening
rain. You better take this scarf.

COHEN

I won't notice the weather, because now I'm healthy and
strong.

(He doesn't take the scarf.)

LOUISE

There are umbrellas by the front door.

COHEN

I love the way you say that.

LOUISE

(She hands him a roll.)

You need to eat. Take a roll.

COHEN

You care about me!

LOUISE

How could I not.

COHEN

Let's study Wagner together! You could be Tristan and I
could be Isolde.

LOUISE

I'll see you at supper.

COHEN

Soon . . . soon.

> *(He exits. Gertrude enters, with a package.)*

GERTRUDE

Who's he?

LOUISE

Someone dangerous. Yesterday he saw what he shouldn't
have seen. And now he's worked his way into the apartment.
They're sharing the room.

GERTRUDE

> *(Delighted.)*

A fantastic intrigue.

LOUISE

And the worst of it is, he suspects Herr Versati's up to something and he swore he'd never allow it.

GERTRUDE

A spoiler.

LOUISE

I'm worried he might blab before anything's had time to happen.

GERTRUDE

What did you do?

LOUISE

I tried to make him feel secure.

GERTRUDE

Expert. And I'll keep an eye on him.

LOUISE

(Indicates the package.)

What's that?

GERTRUDE

The fabric for your new underpants.

(She unwraps it, excitedly.)

LOUISE

It's so soft.

GERTRUDE

Better than silk. I'll make you two pairs. One special, the other very special.

LOUISE

It feels so good against the skin.

GERTRUDE

When these fall down, it will be in the dark of night!

(*Again, they giggle loudly.*)

Let me measure you. [Help me move the bench, I'll need you up a little higher.]

(*Louise hikes up her skirt. Gertrude takes a tape and measures her.*)

LOUISE

Gertrude, you're so beautiful yourself. Why are you doing all this for me?

GERTRUDE

I've given up hope.

LOUISE

No, I won't let you.

GERTRUDE

Do you think there's any point?

LOUISE

Of course, look at you.

GERTRUDE

Oh my god, Louise, it's happening to you now as we speak.

LOUISE

What?

GERTRUDE

Your desire is alive.

LOUISE

Yes ... I have made up my mind. It's the sweetest of dreams already. You can have it, too!

GERTRUDE

Listen to you.

LOUISE

You can, Gertrude. You can.

GERTRUDE

You're making me cry.

LOUISE

Somewhere there's a man for you ... how about the barber boy?

GERTRUDE

I'd rather have your husband.

(They both laugh. Versati enters.)

VERSATI

Aha. Out of the rain I walk into the sun.

LOUISE

(To Gertrude, sotto voce.)

Stay here!

VERSATI

What was so funny?

LOUISE

We were talking about the barber.

VERSATI

What barber?

LOUISE

Your new roommate.

GERTRUDE

Louise was suggesting I take him for a lover.

LOUISE

Gertrude!

GERTRUDE

And . . . for an old maid he's not so bad.

VERSATI

What old maid?

LOUISE

She's fishing for compliments.

GERTRUDE

Only a little.

VERSATI

Compliments must rain over you like petals falling in an
arbor.

GERTRUDE

(Flustered.)

What's your opinion on this fabric?

VERSATI

What's it for?

GERTRUDE

(She points to Louise.)

Panties.

LOUISE

You're unstoppable.

VERSATI

(He holds the fabric, examines it.)

Soft. Sheer. That's nice. Thrilling to touch, but not as thrilling as the skin beneath it.

GERTRUDE

(A-swoon.)

Gee. That touched me in a remote place.

LOUISE

Gertrude . . .

GERTRUDE

(To Versati.)

We were taking measurements.

(Louise is mortified.)

VERSATI

Aha.

GERTRUDE

Around the hips. Quite small hips they are, too. Now I need the length.

(She bends down in front of Louise, and pushes the measuring tape up her skirt.)

LOUISE

Stop it!

VERSATI

May I make a suggestion?

GERTRUDE

What?

VERSATI

Well, you measured quite far down the knee. What's in fashion now is something a little higher.

GERTRUDE

Show us.

(She offers him the tape.)

LOUISE

Gertrude, stop it right now or I'll never forgive you.

(Versati takes the tape and measures up her skirt to her knee.)

VERSATI

The latest fashion is right about here.

(His hand is up her dress, at a point above the knee, improperly high.)

GERTRUDE

I'm going to leave you two alone. But I'll be on the lookout.

VERSATI

He's not due home until three.

GERTRUDE

That's right, you don't know. There's a problem. Someone
else.

VERSATI

Someone else?

GERTRUDE

The barber. He wants to make sure you're never with her.

VERSATI

Aha.

GERTRUDE

I'm going to get more fabric. I hope you enjoy yourselves
while I'm gone.

(She slips out. Versati looks at Louise, approaches her slowly.)

VERSATI

Louise.

LOUISE

(Starts toward him, breathless.)

Yes.

VERSATI

How do you feel?

LOUISE

I'm afraid.

VERSATI

You should be. At this distance, you ignite a warm blue flame in me. Nearer, and I would be razed.

LOUISE

My breath quickens.

VERSATI

Your breasts swell already. I can see the muslin move.

LOUISE

My pulse.

VERSATI

What about it?

LOUISE

(*Rapturously.*)

It exists.

VERSATI

There are so many women, Louise. Pale blondes with subtle streaks of blue along their wrists. Dark-haired, with elegantly

cut figures, tall, short, some wear jangling beads and stones,
or translucent dresses that silhouette in the sun. Some are so
fragile that you touch them like a leaf, some are strong and
you draw them into you forcefully. But you, Louise, are be-
yond category, and when I am with you, I will be in un-
known territory, taking in my hands something unfamiliar
and new, unlike anyone ever. I am on fire, Louise, and there
is no doubt I am finally and forever in love.

LOUISE

Take me.

(But he doesn't. Instead, he keeps talking.)

VERSATI

"Take me." In those two words, our fate. How beautiful
when you say them. If I could capture that feeling on paper,
I would be one of the greats!

LOUISE

Take me.

VERSATI

Take ... take ... I must take up my pen! My inspiration is so
direct, what I write could not come out false.

LOUISE

Take me.

VERSATI

Yes! I will take you and transform you into words.

(He picks up Cohen's scarf, wraps it around Louise's neck.)

And when I am done we will be as tightly woven as this scarf. I the warp and you the weft . . . and then and only then will I demand full payment of your beauty.

(He runs into his room.)

LOUISE

(To the air, her hands rubbing over herself.)

My resistance is gone . . .

(Door slams.)

Hello?

(She goes and listens at Versati's door, confused. She knocks again.)

Herr Versati?

VERSATI

(From behind door, offstage.)

Five minutes, please . . .

(She removes Cohen's scarf, touches it to her face.)

LOUISE

"I the warp and you the weft . . ."

(Cohen appears at the door, sees her, enters. He has a bag of coffee.)

COHEN

You're holding my scarf.

LOUISE

You scared me.

COHEN

You were holding it to your face. Oh my god, Louise. You
miss me so much that when I am gone, you must caress the
artifact!

*(He rushes to her and kisses her, à la Rudolph Valentino. She
dangles for a minute, her arms limp. Cohen stands her back up, then
faints dead away.)*

LOUISE

Oh!

(She goes to him.)

Water.

(She gets water, throws it in his face.)

COHEN

(Coming around.)

Are you all right?

LOUISE

Here, sit up. Ow!

(She pricks her hand on something in his pocket.)

What's in your pocket?

(She retrieves a mechanical drill from his pocket.)

What's this?

COHEN

It's a drill.

LOUISE

Why do you have a drill?

COHEN

It will tell me what's going on in Versati's room.

LOUISE

How?

COHEN

I was going to drill through the divider. To keep an eye on him.

LOUISE

What right do you have!

COHEN

Jealousy gives me the right to be a fool.

(Versati bursts open his door and enters, holding up his pen trium-phantly.)

VERSATI

Triumph! My passion is now fully transcribed onto the page.
Set down in meter and rhyme.

(He reads.)

"Once in place, love never breaks, it is ever fix-ed to the fix-
ing place!" Now I am ready to take you upon my . . .

COHEN

No. You are not ready and you will never be ready.

VERSATI

Who are you?

COHEN

I, sir, am your prophylactic.

VERSATI

Oh, really!

COHEN

And, you might as well know, she has no interest in you.

VERSATI

Tell it to Sappho, you nitwit.

COHEN

I'm a nitwit? You don't have a wit to nit with!

LOUISE

Cohen, you're mad!

COHEN

He's here under false pretenses.

VERSATI

How can a pretense be otherwise?

COHEN

Don't wordsmith me.

(To Louise.)

I've read his poetry. It creaks.

VERSATI

Like your knees.

COHEN

You dye your hair!

VERSATI

I do not!

COHEN

You do too!

VERSATI

Don't.

COHEN

I dyed it.

VERSATI

Well, so did Wagner!

COHEN

(Impressed.)

Wagner dyed your hair?

VERSATI

No, Wagner dyed his own hair.

COHEN

Never!

VERSATI

Absolutely.

COHEN

Wagner wore a wig! Oops!

(He wasn't supposed to reveal that. Cohen covers his mouth.)

LOUISE

Both of you. Stop it!

COHEN

But we are arguing over you!

(Gertrude enters.)

GERTRUDE

Theo's coming!

LOUISE

I will not be won or lost in a fight!

VERSATI

She's right. Her will is independent of us!

COHEN

(Mimics him, in a child's voice.)

"Her will is independent of us." Sycophant!

VERSATI

Wet noodle!

(Cohen attacks Versati; they begin to lightly wrestle.)

COHEN

Plagiarist!

VERSATI

Crybaby!

COHEN

Putz!

GERTRUDE

He's here!

(Theo enters. Cohen and Versati stop wrestling, and all adopt a casual pose.)

THEO

Mealtime!

(Blackout.)

LIGHTS UP. *Dinnertime. Theo, Cohen, and Versati sit around the table, which is covered with the remains of supper. Louise clears plates. They are in the middle of a lively debate.*

THEO

(References the newspaper.)

... that monster in the Loch Ness. Tent cities with thousands of people have sprung up around the lake. All for something imagined.

VERSATI

The imagination is beautiful.

THEO

The imagination rots reality.

VERSATI

It didn't hurt Leonardo.

THEO

Leonardo invented a parachute that doesn't open. Cohen, I stopped by your barbershop today. Your employer had a hard time this afternoon without you. He asked that you be sick on Tuesdays, not Saturdays.

COHEN

It's the first work I've missed in three years. Even a dog will have its rest. Whether or not my boss thinks it's kosher.

THEO

Kosher?

COHEN

Kosher with a *C*.

THEO

Oh. The important thing is to take care of your health.

COHEN

A lot you care.

THEO

How do you mean?

COHEN

Well, for one thing, you gave me a room that faces northeast.

THEO

And?

COHEN

This is exceptionally unhealthy. Everyone knows a room facing northeast is subject to unnatural winds and arctic breezes.
This could exacerbate my condition, whatever it may be.

THEO

Oh, for god's sake. Put the bed opposite the window. You'll
be facing southwest.

COHEN

I never thought of that.

THEO

Here, I'll help you.

(They exit to the bedroom. Louise and Versati are left alone.)

VERSATI

(To Louise.)

You and I will be together tonight. It is written in the stars.

LOUISE

How can we?

VERSATI

I have a plan. I will take Theo out to the boulevard, get
him drunk, and return alone. I will convince him to come
with me.

LOUISE

How? He doesn't seem to like you very much.

VERSATI

At the dinner table I will engage him in a battle of wits and then lure him into a drinking bout.

LOUISE

(Excited.)

He cannot win a battle of wits!

VERSATI

Exactly. I will return in a few hours and make you mine. Will you be ready for me?

LOUISE

I will.

VERSATI

You must take care of Cohen.

LOUISE

But how?

VERSATI

You'll figure out a way. Your participation will heighten your ardor.

LOUISE

Is it wrong what we're doing?

VERSATI

It was God who gave me my passion; it is the devil who prevents it from being spent.

LOUISE

Let's go with God.

(Theo and Cohen reenter from the bedroom.)

THEO

You know, I have a friend with the same complaints as you and he knows his body like an office manual. I asked him about his ailments.

COHEN

What did he say?

THEO

He seems to think it's nerves. But the nerves affect the other organs. The liver, the lungs, the kidneys...

COHEN

Liver, lungs, and kidneys?

LOUISE

You're making Herr Cohen nervous, Theo.

THEO

Exactly my point. Nerves. Too nervous. Affects the liver, lungs, and kidneys.

LOUISE

But he doesn't think he has anything serious.

COHEN

(Nervous.)

I don't have anything serious.

THEO

Then it is my duty to point out the list of possible serious diseases you might have . . . gout, emphysema, whooping cough, mumps, aphasia . . .

COHEN

Stop!

THEO

Meningitis, shingles, measles . . .

COHEN

(More nervous.)

Is there a draft in here?

LOUISE

The window's open a bit.

COHEN

Could we close it?

LOUISE

Here, wear your scarf.

COHEN

(To Louise.)

I . . . I . . . don't know what to say.

VERSATI

May I speak?

THEO

Your rent is paid.

VERSATI

That is the subject of poetry.

(He gestures toward Louise and Cohen.)

See the way a woman's tenderness comforts the sickly and diseased?

THEO

He's not comforted; he feels awful.

COHEN

I am comforted.

VERSATI

My point.

THEO

He's only comforted because he's sick. If he were healthy, he would just be annoyed.

LOUISE

You're not annoyed when I serve you dinner.

THEO

That's because it's a function of duty. It's why when I go off to work you are not annoyed, because I'm doing my duty. And when I am home, it is your duty to serve me dinner. If everyone just did their duty and nothing else, the world would be a better place.

VERSATI

Duty? Is that all you think about? What about the softness of the serving hand? The warm cradle of the female caress? Frocks with frills and polka dots?

THEO

You know what, Versati? You sound like a woman. These are not manly thoughts. A man does not think of polka dots.

VERSATI

I am a man who lives on the poetic side of life.

THEO

A man wields an ax. A man hews wood. He pisses against a
wall. He shoots birds from the air with pellets. He does not
put on brocaded cuff links and stroll off into a garden to
write poetry.

VERSATI

Many men have.

THEO

Yes, I've seen these sensitive "men" singing their hearts out
on the stage, crooning love songs, weeping over their lady
loves. Why would a woman want a man who acts like a
woman? Let women go off and write poetry and stand on
the stage singing of their broken hearts. Men, strong, vital
men, should be at their desks, stamping documents, filing
files and going home at five o'clock.

VERSATI

Monotony!

THEO

Continuity!

VERSATI

Tedium!

THEO

(Rhapsodic.)

Regularity!

VERSATI

It's barbaric!

COHEN

(Indignant.)

How dare you insult barbers!

THEO

Versati, I like where I am. In the middle. I'm proud to have done no better.

VERSATI

Theo, is the woman next to you not enough to motivate you to a higher place?

THEO

How could I be motivated by a little housewife?

LOUISE

I am not a little housewife.

THEO

That's no embarrassment. I have descended from a long line of government clerks. You have descended from a long line of little housewives.

VERSATI

You could be an artist!

THEO

Do you think that if I came home and sang to Louise of my
tender feelings for the heavens she would ever respect me
again?

LOUISE

Yes.

THEO

You just think so.

VERSATI

(To Theo.)

Does the name Nietzsche mean anything to you?

THEO

One of the giants.

VERSATI

You've read him?

THEO

No, I haven't.

VERSATI

Do you want to know what he stands for?

THEO

No thank you.

VERSATI

I'll lend you my copy.

THEO

(Insulted.)

I do not read!

VERSATI

You don't read?

THEO

Never. I work seven hours a day. After that, I'm tired.

VERSATI

So eat, sleep, work. That's your life. And where does it all end?

THEO

With a pension.

VERSATI

And politics doesn't interest you.

THEO

Doesn't affect me.

VERSATI

Science?

THEO

Ho hum.

VERSATI

Theology?

THEO

The stricter the better.

VERSATI

Poetry?

THEO

I'd rather sit on nails.

VERSATI

You disavow the power of poetry? I'll get you a volume.
Promise me you'll read it.

THEO

I'll tell you what. I'll go to the zoo and see the giraffe.

VERSATI

Why?

THEO

Because a giraffe is like a poem. They both make no sense.

VERSATI

Herr Maske, a man is not all muscle. A man is a brain, a heart, a source of sexual power.

THEO

Please do not use such language in this house.

VERSATI

I am referencing Freud!

THEO

I am referencing me!

VERSATI

Herr Maske, a man is only what he contributes to the human race. The heroes are the thinkers, poets, painters, and musicians. And the layperson is only important to the degree that he knows them.

THEO

But what about being a man?

VERSATI

I am a man.

THEO

But no, you're not.

VERSATI

How can you say that?

THEO

Because I know what a man is. There is an essential act of
manhood, and you don't do it.

VERSATI

Oh, there is?

THEO

Yes, there is.

VERSATI

And what is the essential act of manhood?

THEO

A man, a real man, takes care of someone.

(A pause while Versati considers this.)

VERSATI

I take care of someone.

THEO

Yourself doesn't count.

VERSATI

Herr Maske, let me ask you a philosophical question.

THEO

I enjoy a good philosophical question as much as the next
fellow.

COHEN

(Who is sitting next to Theo.)

How would you know that?

THEO

Know what?

COHEN

Well, I am the next fellow and how would you know you
enjoy them as much as I?

THEO

(Ignores him.)

What is it, Versati?

VERSATI

Can you think of any circumstances where it would be all
right for a married woman to have an affair?

(Louise gasps.)

THEO

Of course not.

VERSATI

Why?

THEO

Because only men should have affairs.

VERSATI

And what makes you say that?

THEO

(Turns to Cohen.)

Isn't it in the New Testament or something?

COHEN

Uh yes, I think so ... the book of ... Saint ... Louis.

THEO

Look, my boss's wife was having an affair. He found out about it, but decided to let her. He told everyone he didn't want to infringe on her individual uniqueness. That's where modern thought leads us.

VERSATI

The man's a hero. His wife can look up to him.

LOUISE

His wife despises him.

VERSATI

But he let her express herself.

LOUISE

She despises him from the bottom of her heart.

COHEN

I can settle this. I myself had an affair with a married woman. One night with me and she ran back to her husband. She's been faithful to him ever since.

THEO

But it can't be allowed. It destroys the family.

LOUISE

And what if there is no family?

THEO

The point is, only men can handle it.

VERSATI

(To Theo.)

I can't believe that you believe what you believe.

THEO

I can't change my mind. I'd have nothing to think.

VERSATI

I could change your mind. I could open your heart to the arts.

THEO

Not so.

VERSATI

Might we go out and discuss it over a glass of schnapps?

THEO

Yes, we might.

VERSATI

(Standing, to Louise.)

With your permission?

THEO

Yes, Louise, would you mind if I went to a bar with Versati?

LOUISE

I . . .

THEO

Ha! I'm kidding. Let's go, Versati, I can't wait to hear you stumble and fall. Cohen, you too.

COHEN

I'm tired.

THEO

Suit yourself.

VERSATI

(As they prepare to leave.)

Let me begin. It was Descartes who stated that we exist.

THEO

Someone had to say that?

(They exit. Cohen looks after them.)

COHEN

I suppose you are hot as a pistol after Versati's rhapsody.

LOUISE

(Hesitant.)

No . . .

COHEN

I observed something about him tonight.

LOUISE

What is that?

COHEN

His passion is triggered by the slightest incident.

LOUISE

Like yours.

COHEN

My impulse was to protect. His was to possess.

LOUISE

Oh, please.

COHEN

Why do I get abused around here? You doubt me, Versati hates me, and Theo has been so incredibly cruel to me.

LOUISE

How?

COHEN

He gave me a room facing northeast.

LOUISE

But he moved the bed.

COHEN

Too late. I had already been subjected to infectious viral winds.

(He coughs, or feels a twinge.)

LOUISE

Perhaps you should go lie down.

COHEN

No. Too early.

LOUISE

Take a walk, a long walk.

COHEN

No. The night air would worsen my condition.

LOUISE

I'm not so sure you have a condition.

COHEN

Oh really? Then why, if I have no condition, did my doctor, whom I visited today, upon hearing my symptoms, pre-scribe . . .

(He reaches in his pocket and produces a small vial of pills.)

these.

LOUISE

What are they?

COHEN

They're called . . .

(Reads the label.)

placebos.

LOUISE

You know, you are looking a little pale.

COHEN

Pale?

LOUISE

Let me give you a tonic.

COHEN

What kind of tonic?

LOUISE

A pick-me-up.

(She goes to the kitchen cabinet and gets Gertrude's sleeping mixture.)

COHEN

I'd better not.

LOUISE

Why? It will help.

COHEN

I never mix medicines.

LOUISE

Just a little.

COHEN

No, my doctor warned me against it.

LOUISE

Are you sure? You look ashen.

                    COHEN
I do?

                    LOUISE
Let me look down your throat.

                    COHEN
Why?

              (*She sits him down; he opens his mouth.*)
Is it red?

                    (*She looks.*)

                    LOUISE
Scarlet.

                    COHEN
Feel my glands.

                    LOUISE
Tennis balls.

                    COHEN
Touch my forehead.

              (*She puts her palm on his forehead.*)

                    LOUISE
An inferno!

COHEN

Check my tongue.

(He sticks out his tongue.)

LOUISE

Rabbit fur.

COHEN

Give me the tonic!

LOUISE

Here, take a big gulp.

COHEN

My nerves are failing. One night facing northeast and I'm falling apart.

(He starts to stand.)

Ow! I have no feeling in my legs.

LOUISE

You poor thing.

(He starts off to his bedroom.)

COHEN

No feeling! Do you know how painful it is to have no feeling?

(He gimps off to his bedroom, stiff-legged, stops at the door.)

Boy, I'm suddenly tired.

(He enters the bedroom and closes the door. Louise is alone.)

LOUISE

Well, I'm not just a little housewife after all.

(Gertrude appears outside the glass door. She knocks. Louise opens the door.)

What are you doing up so late?

GERTRUDE

I just came from the comedy. A play by Sternheim. Very funny.

LOUISE

Should I see it?

GERTRUDE

Wait till it's adapted.

(Then, excited.)

Are we alone?

LOUISE

We are.

GERTRUDE

So. This afternoon, with Versati . . .

(She grabs Louise's hands and stares into her face.)

LOUISE

What?

GERTRUDE

I want to drink in your happiness. I want to see the light
dancing in your eyes. Tell me. What happened? Every detail
for your guardian. How did it get started?

LOUISE

Well, he stood over there.

GERTRUDE

Oh my god.

> (She runs to the spot, feels the air with her hands.)

There's still heat here! Where were you?

LOUISE

Near the bedroom.

GERTRUDE

Then he came to you.

LOUISE

He stayed where he was.

GERTRUDE

And?

LOUISE

Talked.

GERTRUDE

Perfect. He seduced you by words alone.

LOUISE

He said he was finally and forever in love.

GERTRUDE

That unlocks the legs. Then what happened. He neared you.

LOUISE

Yes. Closer and closer.

GERTRUDE

He makes lightning shoot through you, and in the face of his masculine power your body is weak.

LOUISE

I lost all my senses.

GERTRUDE

Louise!

LOUISE

Then he came to me.

GERTRUDE

And?

                    LOUISE
Talked.

                    GERTRUDE
And?

                    LOUISE
Spoke.

                    GERTRUDE
And?

                    LOUISE
Talked.

                    GERTRUDE
And after he had said it all?

                    LOUISE
He left.

                    GERTRUDE
Did what?

                    LOUISE
Left.

                    GERTRUDE
He left? Where did he go?

LOUISE

To his room.

GERTRUDE

And you followed him in!

LOUISE

No.

GERTRUDE

Because?

LOUISE

He locked himself in.

GERTRUDE

So nothing happened?

LOUISE

No.

GERTRUDE

Then why do you look so happy?

LOUISE

He wrote a poem to me, swearing his love forever. And he's coming back tonight.

GERTRUDE

Aha.

LOUISE

He has a plan. He's out right now getting Theo drunk.

GERTRUDE

And Cohen?

LOUISE

I gave him your sleeping medicine. I told him it was a tonic.

(*Gertrude starts to cry.*)

Why are you crying?

GERTRUDE

Deception, lying, trickery, my little girl is all grown up.

(*She goes over to Louise and hugs her, then breaks.*)

I wonder why he behaved so strangely this afternoon.

LOUISE

Strangely?

GERTRUDE

A man will not put off to tomorrow what he can sleep with today.

(*She thinks.*)

Well, of course.

LOUISE

What?

GERTRUDE

Cohen must have been here, hiding, spying on you.

LOUISE

He wasn't. He walked in right afterward.

GERTRUDE

Aha.

LOUISE

That is a bit odd.

GERTRUDE

Darling, he noticed Cohen spying. He delayed his grati-
fication for your honor. He galloped to his room with balls
of blue. He sat at his desk like a unicorn . . . the ink from
his pen pulsing onto the paper. All to keep Cohen from
knowing.

LOUISE

Do you think?

GERTRUDE

Louise, you're young. You don't know the machinations a
man will go through for a woman. It's a great show; enjoy it.
Tonight at the comedy, I saw a man climb walls, fight duels,
all for a woman he wanted. For all his effort you must reward him. When Versati comes through that door tonight,
you must be ready. I'll be your lookout . . . If your husband
comes home while he's here, I'll bang three times.

(She stamps her foot three times to illustrate.)

Amore . . .

(She exits. Louise is left alone in the room.)

LOUISE

(Softly.)

Amore.

(She locks Cohen's door. She begins to undress in the dim light. Down to her slip and panties. There is noise on the stairwell. Footsteps. She stands, vulnerable, open, waiting. Theo enters. Sees her.)

THEO

Louise. What if a man came in!

(There are three loud bangs. Theo exits to the bedroom. Louise is left alone onstage to lament. Blackout.)

THE NEXT MORNING. *Dirty plates from breakfast are on the table, a single place setting. Theo is in the living room, in shirtsleeves and suspenders. He talks to Louise, who is in the bedroom.*

THEO

This is a sloppy job you did mending my suspenders. I hope you're not servicing these men at my expense. And what were you doing last night, standing in the living room? Practicing to have your panties fall down? Thank god neither of our boarders is around. Cohen hasn't stirred, and Versati won't be here till after lunch. I can guarantee you that.

LOUISE

What happened to him? He didn't come home last night.

THEO

He kept making a point and ordering a drink. He would say something incomprehensible, and triumphantly demand another round. For every one I drank, he drank two. My body is thick, and the alcohol settles in the legs. His is thin and it quickly rises above the eyes. [My body is hard and the muscles resist the alcohol. His is soft and absorbs it like a sponge.]

LOUISE

Where did he disappear to? Did he need to go write?

THEO

How should I know? I must say, I'm pretty good at this philosophical debate. I cornered him a few times.

LOUISE

Where did he sleep?

THEO

Who knows. But I think that whatever brought him here has evaporated. Where's the sugar?

LOUISE

We're out.

THEO

Out. I want to stop nagging you, but you won't let me. What about Cohen?

LOUISE

He complained about his room facing northeast again.

THEO

The man's insane. What, are north and east inferior parts of the sky? For a miserable twelve taler he wants me to throw in south and west?

(Louise opens the door to Versati's room, peers in.)

LOUISE

Versati's things are still here. He has to return. Doesn't he?

THEO

The man vanished like a vapor. One minute in my face; the next he was gone. I drank too much last night and now I've got a sloppy, drunken diarrhea. I'm amazed you could sleep with all my trips to the toilet.

LOUISE

But a man wouldn't just stay out all night if he had other obligations . . .

THEO

Oh my dear, you are naive.

LOUISE

(Thoughtful.)

Yes, I suppose I am.

(Then.)

I'd like to go to church today.

THEO

Stay here. I need you around.

LOUISE

Theo, I don't ask for much. I want out of the house, just for a few hours.

THEO

No, Your place is here. And don't bother me, I'm trying to sort out something that's been rattling around in my head.

LOUISE

What?

(Louise begins to get dressed to go out.)

THEO

Curious? You might be amazed. Just give me an hour to think about it. In fact, I need to be alone. Why don't you go off to church? It's a good place for you to be seen. And someone's got to atone for your dropped panties.

LOUISE

I was going anyway.

THEO

No more ladies' magazines for you!

(Louise readies to leave. Cohen enters from the bedroom, spry.)

COHEN

What a sleep! Either that or a coma.

THEO

You're up late. You missed breakfast.

COHEN

I was out cold. I fell asleep on my hand and when I woke up
I was still on it. It was as though I had been drugged!

(This stops him; he looks at Louise, but he dismisses the idea.)

LOUISE

I'm off.

THEO

Mention my name. God likes me.

(She exits.)

So you slept well. You must like the room.

COHEN

No, I hate the room.

THEO

So you want to move.

COHEN

No, I want a year's lease.

THEO

Cohen, you are bizarre.

COHEN

Versati has a year's lease; as long as Versati's here, I'm here.

THEO

Rents are rising around here. In two months it's worth fifteen.

COHEN

Twelve. We agreed. And where's the sugar?

THEO

Fourteen and no sugar.

COHEN

Thirteen. And I want sugar!

THEO

In advance. And no sugar.

COHEN

That's my savings!

THEO

Going . . . going . . .

COHEN

All right. To have it done with.

(He takes out his checkbook. Theo goes to a drawer and retrieves a form.)

THEO

Let's sign.

(Cohen starts writing his check.)

COHEN

I can't believe that a man who uttered the names of Luther and Schiller could do something like this.

THEO

(Reading from the form.)

For one year . . .

(He writes his name.)

Herr Maske leases to . . .

(Writes.)

Herr Cohen . . . oops, that should be with a *K* . . .

(Cohen corrects the spelling of his name on the check. Theo reads again.)

One room including morning coffee . . .

(Writes.)

Without sugar.

COHEN

With!

THEO

Without!

COHEN

Give me that.

(He angrily signs, hands Theo the check.)

I'm going out to get some sugar.

THEO

Leave it in the kitchen where we can all use it.

(Cohen exits.)

Gee, it was just a whim to ask him for more. I'm stunned that he did it. Hmm. Twenty-eight taler altogether, times twelve, is 336 taler a year. I make six hundred, that's 936. Our expenses are 950, 960. Hmm. We're almost living for free.

(Gertrude comes to the door, knocks. She is holding a package.)

Come in.

GERTRUDE

Is your wife here?

THEO

At church.

GERTRUDE

Herr Versati?

THEO

They're all out.

GERTRUDE

Oh.

(She starts to go.)

THEO

What's that? You're hiding something.

GERTRUDE

A package ... nothing.

(He approaches her, playfully, grabs the package.)

THEO

You're pretty today, Gertrude.

GERTRUDE

I don't believe you.

THEO

If a man says it, at that moment it is true.

(Theo opens the package. They are panties. He holds them up.)

Well. Silk and lace. Anyone who wears these is asking to be taken seriously.

GERTRUDE

They're not mine. They're a gift to Louise.

THEO

You would look beautiful in these.

GERTRUDE

You think so?

THEO

Old ships don't hoist silk sails.

GERTRUDE

Meaning?

THEO

(Holds up the underpants.)

If you had these on, you would be irresistible.

GERTRUDE

Herr Maske!

THEO

Oh, don't think that I haven't noticed that you are ... of sound bottom.

GERTRUDE

I didn't know you were like this!

THEO

You don't know me at all. I know you've never thought much of me. And I let you, because so what. But today you came along in that dress, and now with these ...

GERTRUDE

I was just going to fit them on your wife.

THEO

You know who's in and out in this building. Louise is at church. You must have seen her leave.

GERTRUDE

I'm taken aback.

THEO

A euphemism for "from behind"?

(Gertrude gasps.)

And I don't think this is so shocking to you.

GERTRUDE

What makes you say that?

THEO

You haven't left.

GERTRUDE

If Louise knew about this . . .

THEO

I'll never tell her, because it would hurt her. But I've done it before, not often, but with pleasure.

GERTRUDE

A man is, in the end, a man.

THEO

Only since my voice changed.

GERTRUDE

How could we look her in the eye?

THEO

Desire adjusts morality.

GERTRUDE

You might not like me. I'm forty-two.

THEO

Rivers still flow from rusty pipes.

GERTRUDE

That's the most romantic thing anyone's ever said to me.

THEO

I want to sleep with you. It won't take a minute.

GERTRUDE

I'm torn. On one hand, yes. And on the other, why not.

(Theo puts his hand on her rear.)

Don't touch me there . . .

THEO

Here?

GERTRUDE

Better.

THEO

Come into the bedroom.

GERTRUDE

Are you finally and forever in love?

THEO

With what?

GERTRUDE

(Disappointment.)

Oh.

THEO

I'll be in the room. I am going to take off my pants. When you come in, I'll have a little surprise for you.

(He exits.)

GERTRUDE

Little?

(She takes the underpants, goes to the door, stands, trying to make up her mind. Klinglehoff enters; Gertrude doesn't see him.)

No, the devil will find me.

(She turns, sees Klinglehoff, screams.)

GERTRUDE

Who are you?

KLINGLEHOFF

I'm here to rent a room.

GERTRUDE

The landlord's not available right now. Could you amuse yourself for a few minutes?

KLINGLEHOFF

I don't like being amused. I'll wait around the corner.

(He exits. Gertrude looks back at Theo's room.)

GERTRUDE

Oh Louise, someone will rob you of your innocence, but it won't be me.

(She takes the underpants and rewraps them, leaving the package where Louise can see them. She exits.)

THEO

(Enters from the bedroom in his underpants, refers to his groin.)

Damn it, Gertrude, the moment passed.

(Theo realizes Gertrude is not there. Versati enters.)

VERSATI

Ah, good, you're home. In your underpants.

THEO

It's a tradition around here.

(He returns to his room and gets dressed.)

VERSATI

I can't wait to tell you what happened after I left. You will be amazed. While you were staggering home . . .

THEO

I had gas. Home is the only place for passing gas.

VERSATI

Well, I hate to say it, but you challenged me. The philosophy of my life suddenly under question.

THEO

(False modesty.)

Please. I'm an assistant clerk.

VERSATI

You were such an event for me. Theo the bureaucrat, a life-
altering encounter. I paced the riverbank up and down,
thinking, thinking about what you said. Then, I noticed a
shadowy figure.

THEO

A thief?

VERSATI

A woman. An angel. We exchanged rapturous glances. Not
of lust, but of mind. And suddenly I knew you were right.

THEO

About what?

VERSATI

A man must take care of someone. So, I followed her home.
And there, in the dim candlelight, she poured forth her
goodness, her spirit; in short, her soul. I fell to my knees.
And bowed down before her. Every day she offers her body
to anybody, but when she comes home, she dwells in the land
of divine spirit.

THEO

A prostitute. Nothing wrong with that. I admire the workingman.

VERSATI

I can't sleep. I can't sleep until I take care of someone. See
that she is clothed, fed. I will cook for her, clean
for her.

THEO

You have it backwards.

VERSATI

And write her down on paper. I shall filter her image
through my heart and write a sonnet, an ode...

(Aside.)

Perhaps a quatrain with an added pentameter... the academy
would be shocked.

(Back to Theo.)

Each night I shall read to her, elevate her soul, and we shall
dwell in the clouds.

THEO

Versati, you have performed a miracle.

VERSATI

How's that?

THEO

You have utterly changed your beliefs and yet your actions
remain the same.

VERSATI

Yes! It is the mark of a politician. I'm going to get a place near her. I have never been so motivated by a woman.

THEO

But you have a year's contract.

VERSATI

I won't break it. I'll pay it all right now.

(He takes out some cash and puts it on the table.)

And go ahead and rent it out to someone else. I'll pick up my things later.

THEO

There's six taler too many.

VERSATI

Keep it.

THEO

May I say, you're inexplicable.

VERSATI

All I am is a man of action. I am drawn irresistibly toward that woman. In a few months, I will send you my masterpiece.

(He goes toward the door. Klinglehoff appears.)

Good-bye, good friend. In the world of jam, you are a mar-
malade. I must write that down . . .

(He exits, leaving the door open. Klinglehoff enters.)

THEO

Who are you?

KLINGLEHOFF

Someone told me there was a room here for rent.

THEO

Ah, come in!

KLINGLEHOFF

When will the landlord be available? I must interview everyone thoroughly.

THEO

I am the landlord and you're in luck. A room just came free.
Sixteen taler, including breakfast.

KLINGLEHOFF

Are there any children in the building? Tubas in the building? Sewing machines, parrots? Banjos?

THEO

None.

KLINGLEHOFF

You're married?

                    THEO
Yes.

                  KLINGLEHOFF
Is your wife young?

                    THEO
She is.

                  KLINGLEHOFF
Flirtatious? I wouldn't be happy with that.

                    THEO
She's not.

                  KLINGLEHOFF
You stay on your guard? I don't want men around.

                    THEO
I am never fooled.

                  KLINGLEHOFF
Very well. Any personal contact must be avoided. Your wife,
when she's doing her duties, must, before entering, knock
three times. She must wear decent clothing, not ripped or re-
vealing. There must be no salacious talk, implications, or otherwise questionable innuendo. Instead of coffee, I'll take tea.
Coffee stimulates. When I get excited I have been known to
utter a foul string of obscenities. I'd rather avoid that. I suffer
from constipation, but that's my business.

THEO

Yes, it is.

KLINGLEHOFF

I'll try the room for a month. My name's Klinglehoff, I'm a
scientist. My things will be delivered here promptly.

THEO

I will need a contract. Let me get my papers. Sit there.

*(Klinglehoff sits in the corner of the room. Theo heads toward his
bedroom. Enter Cohen, who sees Klinglehoff.)*

COHEN

There. Sugar. Who is that?

KLINGLEHOFF

Klinglehoff!

THEO

He's a new tenant. He's staying here.

COHEN

Where?

THEO

In Versati's room. He has just checked out.

COHEN

What?

THEO

Versati paid in advance and left.

COHEN

He left?

THEO

Gone.

COHEN

Why?

THEO

Some woman he met.

COHEN

What woman?

THEO

A woman he met on the street.

(Theo exits to the bedroom.)

COHEN

A woman he met on the street?

(Aside.)

With Versati gone, I have no use here. I cannot protect those who are not under threat. Herr Maske!

(Theo enters with papers.)

I'm leaving.

> THEO

You're going, too?

> COHEN

I'll pick up my things later. I'm keeping the sugar. And, I want a refund of my rent.

> THEO

A deal's a deal. You said so yourself.

> COHEN

I'll call my lawyer.

> THEO

You don't have a lawyer.

> COHEN

I'll become one!

> THEO

If the room rents, I'll refund. Otherwise, nothing.

> COHEN

All right. I'm leaving this house. But may I say, Herr Maske, not only am I Cohen with a *C* . . .

(Theo reacts with a sharp intake of breath. So does Klinglehoff.)

But I thoroughly enjoyed, in fact relished in the delight, of seeing a certain view in the park the other day, and it wasn't of all the King's horses and all the King's men . . . but something much more wonderful!

THEO

What? Cohen with a *C*!?

COHEN

I shall return tomorrow morning to gather my things.

(Louise enters.)

Good day, Frau Maske.

(He exits.)

THEO

Louise, take care of him. I have paperwork to do.

(He exits to the bedroom. Louise takes off her scarf and coat. She turns, sees Klinglehoff.)

LOUISE

(Huffy.)

Well. Who are you?

KLINGLEHOFF

I am one who prefers the formal to the familiar and, therefore, would appreciate a less aggressive inquiry.

LOUISE

Well, sir, you're in my house and I would like to know who you are.

KLINGLEHOFF

I am your new tenant.

LOUISE

Our flat is fully rented.

KLINGLEHOFF

Not anymore, evidently.

LOUISE

Since when?

KLINGLEHOFF

Since today. Your husband is drawing up a contract as we speak.

(She goes to the bedroom door.)

LOUISE

Theo?

(Theo pokes his head through the door, a half-drawn contract in his hand.)

THEO

You're late. Did you confess at church?

LOUISE

Yes.

THEO

I hope it did you good.

LOUISE

The priest made me tell the story over and over. After the sixth retelling, I received complete forgiveness.

THEO

That's a relief.

(He starts to go.)

LOUISE

Cohen's gone?

THEO

And Herr Versati. Checked out.

LOUISE

Versati? Did they say why?

THEO

Cohen was enigmatic and Versati was insane. Something about meeting a woman and being swept off his feet.

LOUISE

A woman? What woman?

THEO

Someone he met last night. Said he had never been so moved by a woman before. Said he wanted to write poems to her.

LOUISE

Oh.

(He retreats into the bedroom. She takes the poem Versati gave her from her bosom and reads it.)

"Once in place, love never breaks."

(She takes the poem to the stove and throws it in, then turns and glares at Klinglehoff. She walks toward him.)

So you're just another man applying for a room in our house.

KLINGLEHOFF

That is why I'm here.

LOUISE

Yes, you're just looking for a room, I suppose, to do your work. A room to get away from it all.

KLINGLEHOFF

Exactly.

LOUISE

To pursue with diligence whatever is your area of interest, which is, in this case, let's see, poetry? A quiet study of the arts?

KLINGLEHOFF

In fact, science.

LOUISE

Ah, science. And I wonder if perhaps you were in the park the other day for the King's parade?

KLINGLEHOFF

It is one's patriotic duty.

LOUISE

Under a linden tree?

KLINGLEHOFF

Linden trees line the boulevard.

LOUISE

And what did you see?

KLINGLEHOFF

Something wonderful!

LOUISE

So it's just coincidence, is it, that you came here, to this place, to seek a room next to a famous pair of underpants.

KLINGLEHOFF

How dare you!

LOUISE

(Her voice rising.)

Oh, please. Now that I've learned to read a man's face, I can see that lust is written all over yours.

(Klinglehoff turns toward audience, mulls this.)

KLINGLEHOFF

Madam, I have no idea what you are talking about!

LOUISE

Oh really? Well, does this ring any bells?

(She lifts up her skirt high and shows him her underpants.)

KLINGLEHOFF

Oh my Lord High Chancellor!

(There is a pause.)

LOUISE

Did you say you don't know what I'm talking about?

KLINGLEHOFF

I swear it! I don't know!

LOUISE

But you said you saw something wonderful.

KLINGLEHOFF

The King! I saw the King.

LOUISE

Then, you really don't know?

KLINGLEHOFF

Let me just say that this is the kind of conversation that I have avoided my entire life. I have not only left rooms, but countries that have tried to engage me in perversity. And I cannot believe that filth of this kind has penetrated into the very heart of the German home! You are behaving like, like an American.

(Louise suddenly changes her tone to friendly.)

LOUISE

You're here to rent a room?

KLINGLEHOFF

(Struck by her sudden change.)

Pardon me?

LOUISE

You're here to rent a room?

KLINGLEHOFF

I was.

LOUISE

And you changed your mind?

KLINGLEHOFF

Most undoubtedly.

LOUISE

May I ask why?

KLINGLEHOFF

Why? Because a few seconds ago, you lifted your dress over
your head!

LOUISE

(Feigning shock.)

I did what?

KLINGLEHOFF

You lifted your dress over your head!

LOUISE

I have to ask you. Are you subject to delusions?

KLINGLEHOFF

What do you mean?

LOUISE

Do you ever misplace things?

KLINGLEHOFF

On occasion.

LOUISE

Ever go to the market and forget why you went?

KLINGLEHOFF

Sometimes. Age does that.

LOUISE

Yes, age can do that. As well as make one believe that someone has lifted her dress over her head.

KLINGLEHOFF

You're saying you didn't?

LOUISE

I assure you it's not in my nature. I just came back from
church. But I forgive you.

KLINGLEHOFF

Well then, my dear lady, I apologize.

LOUISE

That's all right, it's quite a common symptom of genius.

KLINGLEHOFF

Oh yes, I'm sure I've heard that. I think I need to rest.
Would you tell your husband that I'll come by tomorrow
to sign the contract, and that my things will be here at
week's end?

LOUISE

I will, Herr . . .

KLINGLEHOFF

Klinglehoff.

LOUISE

Herr Klinglehoff.

KLINGLEHOFF

I'm sorry if I offended you.

LOUISE

Don't think about it. Go off and rest.

(He exits. Theo enters from the bedroom.)

THEO

Where is he?

LOUISE

He said he will come by tomorrow to sign. He wasn't feeling well.

THEO

He'd better. We already have a verbal agreement.

LOUISE

He seemed sincere.

THEO

And what would you know about it?

LOUISE

Nothing, of course. What would you like to eat?

THEO

(Somewhat mysterious.)

That pork chop you've been saving. Tonight's a special night.

LOUISE

What do you mean?

THEO

How long have we been married?

LOUISE

One year today.

THEO

Oh yes, happy anniversary. Do you know that the two gentle-
men, who stumbled by chance into our house, and now en-
hanced by a third—do you know what they've done?

LOUISE

I don't know.

THEO

Can't you guess? They've made it possible for us to have a
baby. We can finally afford it. What do you think?

LOUISE

Of course.

(She goes over to the window, stares out.)

THEO

I send you a kiss in celebration. We can start in a few
minutes. It shouldn't take long. Every evening before supper
until the job is done. Oh and by the way, I want the pork
chop rare! Put butter on it.

(He paces about the room.)

The dishes need washing. The clock needs winding.
The floor needs cleaning. You should see the priest every
Sunday and midweek, too, for a while. Whoa, I've got gas.

(He heads toward the bedroom.)

And look at this . . .

(He reads the headline.)

The monster in the Loch Ness has vanished. The tourists
have left, and the economy is down. Ha. The crowds come
and go, quick to move on to the next sensational thing. I'll
get ready. Come and see me in a few minutes.

*(He exits. She looks toward the bedroom. She touches her belly. She
goes to the package and picks up Gertrude's fancy underwear. She
holds them up to her, then enters the bedroom. Blackout.)*

MORNING. *Lights up on Louise sitting at the kitchen table. She
is thoughtful, moody. There is a rap at the door.*

LOUISE

Come in?

(Cohen pokes his head in.)

COHEN

Oh. I'm sorry to bother; I've come back for my things.

LOUISE

I can help you.

COHEN

I couldn't ask you to. I can do it.

LOUISE

Sit then. Would you like some coffee?

COHEN

I would. Thank you.

(Louise pours him coffee. He sits.)

I'm sorry Versati is gone.

LOUISE

How can you say that?

COHEN

Sorry for you. I know you liked him.

LOUISE

That's the odd thing. I didn't.

                    COHEN

I understand.

                    LOUISE

You do?

                    COHEN

We were all caught in a trap of circumstance.

                    LOUISE

How so?

                    COHEN

This event, this failure of a knot in a string, catapulted us
into rare air. Our desires became disconnected from this
earth. Versati motivated by fantasy, myself motivated by jealousy. Your mind clouded by romance.

                    LOUISE

Why did you leave?

                    COHEN

I suppose my jealousy finally exhausted itself. I longed to
come down to earth. My normal life wasn't so bad.

                    LOUISE

The most peculiar result of all this, is that I'm now with my
husband.

                    COHEN

Ah.

                        LOUISE
He has reclaimed me.

                        COHEN
Just so. Still, it's strange.

                        LOUISE
But there is something even more strange.

                        COHEN
My leaving?

                        LOUISE
No, though you have meant something to me.

                        COHEN
Versati's sudden reversal?

                        LOUISE
No, Versati is a man of reversals. It is something else, something that leaves me surprisingly empty.

                        COHEN
May I ask what it is?

                        LOUISE
My fame is gone.

                        COHEN
Ah.

LOUISE

I was so desired.

COHEN

Yes . . .

LOUISE

But over nothing. An accident. Everyone wanted to be near me. I was notorious. But they left as quickly as they came.

COHEN

You have real worth, Louise. But our eyes were drawn into the dirt.

(She hugs him. Theo enters.)

THEO

Cohen, she is occupied territory.

COHEN

Good morning, Herr Maske. I just came to pick up my things.

THEO

Well, Louise is not one of them.

COHEN

(Testy.)

It was just a friendly good-bye.

(He starts to leave.)

THEO

Hold on, Cohen; let me say one thing to you. I will miss you.

COHEN

Miss me?

THEO

Yes. You stirred things up around here in a most unpleasant way. But it was still lively and I like you for it. Which proves one thing.

COHEN

What is that?

THEO

The individual is not indicative of the group.

COHEN

In your case, Herr Maske, the individual *is* indicative of the group.

(Klinglehoff enters.)

KLINGLEHOFF

Excuse me, I've come to sign my papers.

THEO

Ah yes. Cohen, Herr Klinglehoff is your replacement. I don't think he'll be dancing any jigs, but he's an interesting fellow.

KLINGLEHOFF

I'd rather be dead than interesting.

(Gertrude enters. She has a package.)

GERTRUDE

I have a surprise for you.

(She unfurls a pair of fancy underpants, made with the colors of the German flag, and holds them high.)

THEO

Well! Splendid!

GERTRUDE

Do you like them?

LOUISE

Oh yes, they're lovely.

THEO

I can feel movement down below. How can you be so calm, Klinglehoff?

KLINGLEHOFF

Because I know this is not happening.

LOUISE

Herr Klinglehoff, don't you like Gertrude's German flag?

KLINGLEHOFF

It's beautiful and I salute it.

(He does.)

GERTRUDE

Oh, someone's coming.

THEO

Perhaps Versati. To ask for his rent money.

GERTRUDE

No. The footsteps are too heavy [or light, depending on the actor] for Versati.

LOUISE

We're not expecting anyone.

COHEN

The "For Rent" sign is out of the window.

(The footsteps increase. The cast is at attention. Finally, an elegant man enters, dressed in full regalia. The cast sees him, and they all fall to one knee.)

KLINGLEHOFF

Oh my Lord, it's the King!

THEO

(To Louise.)

I told you this would happen!

(Klinglehoff leans over to Gertrude, takes the new underpants from her and lays them across his arms as though he were presenting a flag, and supplicates himself before the King. The King looks bewildered.)

KLINGLEHOFF

Your Lordship.

KING

Please rise. Is this the home of Theo Maske?

THEO

Yes, it is. I assure that what happened the other day . . .

KING

I have heard of your work, Herr Maske. How thorough you are. How concerned with detail. You are a blessing to the German people as well as an asset to the King.

THEO

I . . .

KING

Once every several years, I like to visit my administrators and reward them personally. And I am pleased to tell you, Herr Maske, that you are being promoted to assistant Over Clerk in the King's personal offices.

THEO

Oh, Your Highness, to think that word of my dedication reached your ears is reward enough.

KING

Herr Maske, I shake your hand.

(He does.)

If only there were more citizens like you, our society would tick like a German clock.

THEO

Thank you, Your Highness.

KING

It is I who salute you, as a servant of the German State. Good-bye.

(He starts to exit.)

Oh, one other thing. I was wondering if you have a room for rent. I'm looking for something small, where I can get a little work done . . . nothing much, a little place to get away, to perhaps write poetry.

THEO

Why, Your Majesty, I'm sure that could be arranged.

KING

I'll have my men deliver some rubber goods tonight.

(They all bow to him as they leave.)

COHEN

I'm checking back in.

(Gertrude runs for the exit.)

THEO

Where are you going?

GERTRUDE

I can hear better from upstairs.

(She exits.)

KLINGLEHOFF

What about me? There are no rooms left!

THEO

You'll share with the King.

KLINGLEHOFF

(Excited.)

Thundering pussy ass balls!

THEO

Louise, go and ready the King's room!

(She turns to him but doesn't move.)

Louise, I said get the King's room ready!

(She stands, walks to her room.)

LOUISE

(In control.)

In my own good time.

(She strolls to her bedroom. Theo stands shocked. Gertrude smiles. Blackout.)